Sticker Fun
with
Hairy Maclary

Lynley Dodd

PUFFIN

Hairy Maclary and friends

Puffing and panting
impatient to see,
together they came
to the foot of the tree.

Find stickers of Bottomley Potts,
Hairy Maclary and Schnitzel von Krumm
and put them under the tree.

With a bellicose bark
and a boisterous bounce,
Hairy Maclary
was ready
to
POUNCE.

*Find the sticker of an angry
Scarface Claw and put him face
to face with Hairy Maclary.*

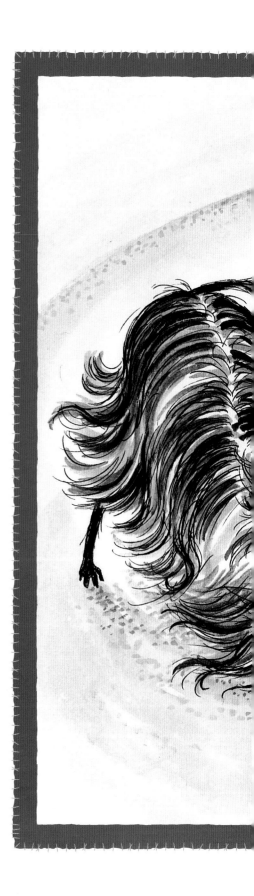

Scarface Claw

Bottomley Potts

Galloping here,
galloping there,
rollicking,
frolicking,

EVERYWHERE.

*Find stickers of a leaping
Bottomley Potts and a flying
duck and put them in the picture.*

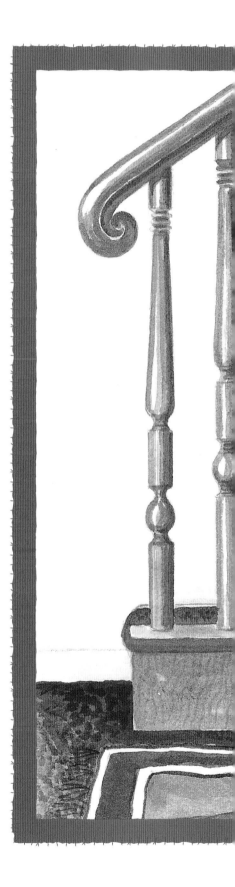

Tucked in a hideyhole
under the stair,
lay a rickety basket
in need of repair.

*Can you find a sticker of
Schnitzel von Krumm asleep in his
basket and put him under the stairs?*

Schnitzel von Krumm

Zachary Quack

Pittery pattery,
skittery scattery,

ZIP

round the corner
came
Zachary Quack.

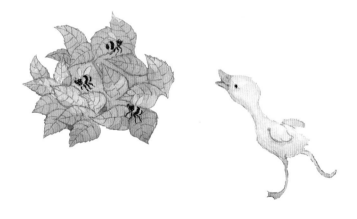

Can you find stickers of little
Zachary Quack and a group of
buzzy bees to add to the picture?

They tangled the towels
and hung on a rope,
they paddled in powder
and slid on
the soap.

*Can you find stickers of Slinky Malinki's
pawprints in the powder and Stickybeak Syd
sliding along on a bar of soap?
Add them to the picture!*

Slinky Malinki and Stickybeak Syd

Greywacke Jones

Greywacke Jones
was hunting a bee.
BUT ALONG CAME
HAIRY MACLARY . . .
and chased her up high
in the sycamore tree.

*Find a sticker of a scared Greywacke Jones
and make her hide at the top of the tree!*

Scarface Claw bothered
and bustled him,
rustled and hustled him,
raced him
and chased him
ALL the way
home.

*Can you find a sticker of Scarface Claw
and make him chase after Hairy Maclary?*

Scarface Claw

Slinky Malinki

Slinky Malinki
was down in the reeds.
BUT ALONG CAME
HAIRY MACLARY . . .
and hustled him into
a drum full of weeds.

*Find a sticker of Slinky Malinki
and make him slink through the reeds!*

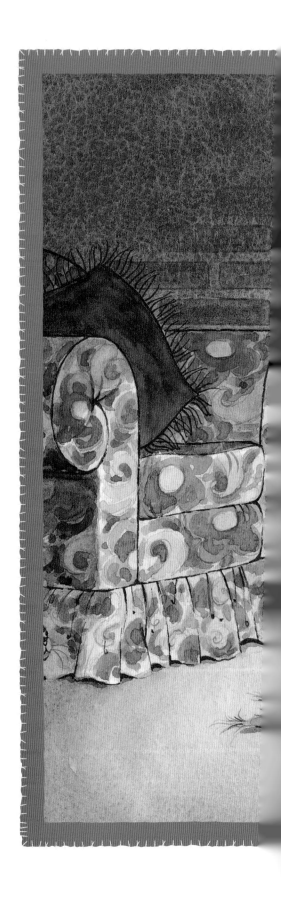

Slinky Malinki
was cosy and snug,
with all of his friends
on the raggedy
rug.

*Find a sticker of Slinky Malinki and four
little kittens and sit them in front of the fire.*

Slinky Malinki and friends

Hairy Maclary and friends

Off with a yowl
a wail and a howl,
a scatter of paws
and a clatter of claws . . .

*Find a sticker of Hairy Maclary's
five friends and make them
run away too!*

PUFFIN BOOKS

Published by the Penguin Group
Penguin Books Ltd, 80 Strand, London WC2R 0RL, England
Penguin Group (USA) Inc., 375 Hudson Street, New York, New York 10014, USA
Penguin Group (Canada), 10 Alcorn Avenue, Toronto, Ontario, Canada M4V 3B2 (a division of Pearson Penguin Canada Inc.)
Penguin Ireland, 25 St Stephen's Green, Dublin 2, Ireland (a division of Penguin Books Ltd)
Penguin Group (Australia), 250 Camberwell Road, Camberwell, Victoria 3124, Australia (a division of Pearson Australia Group Pty Ltd)
Penguin Books India Pvt Ltd, 11 Community Centre, Panchsheel Park, New Delhi – 110 017, India
Penguin Group (NZ), cnr Airborne and Rosedale Roads, Albany, Auckland 1310, New Zealand (a division of Pearson New Zealand Ltd)
Penguin Books (South Africa) (Pty) Ltd, 24 Sturdee Avenue, Rosebank, Johannesburg 2196, South Africa

Penguin Books Ltd, Registered Offices: 80 Strand, London WC2R 0RL, England

puffinbooks.com

Material first published by Mallinson Rendel Publishers Ltd 1983, 1985, 1987, 1993, 1994, 1997, 1998, 1999
This edition first published by Puffin Books 2005
5 6 7 8 9 10

Set in GillSans
Manufactured in China

British Library Cataloguing in Publication Data
A CIP catalogue record for this book is available from the British Library

ISBN 978-0-141-50040-9